BLUE ROSE

THE GUARDIAN'S QUEST

ABHINAY KRISHNA

Made with ❤ on the Notion Press Platform
www.notionpress.com

To,

Those who dared to dream.

Contents

FOREWORD

Prepare to be swept away by "Blue Rose," a tale of mystery, betrayal, and the unwavering power of friendship.

KD's life takes an unexpected turn when he accidentally unleashes Zina, a radiant being from another world, from her centuries-long imprisonment. Thrust into a realm of ancient prophecies and otherworldly powers, KD must navigate a treacherous path, where danger lurks in every shadow.

"The Blue Rose" weaves a gothic story of suspense and wonder. KD's journey is a testament to the strength of the human spirit, a reminder that even in the darkest of times, hope flickers like a distant flame.

Preface

"Blue Rose" was born from a fascination with the gothic, a love for the macabre, and a desire to explore the hidden corners of reality. It's a story that blends the mundane with the extraordinary, the ordinary with the otherworldly.

Within these pages, you'll find a world where ancient prophecies intertwine with modern-day struggles, where the supernatural collides with the all-too-human. It's a world of secrets, betrayal, and sacrifice, where friendships are tested and destinies are forged.

So, step into the shadows, dear reader, and let the story unfold.

Acknowledgements

I am deeply grateful to the many people who supported me throughout the writing of this book. To my family and friends, thank you for your unwavering encouragement and belief in my dreams. And to my readers, thank you for taking this journey with me.

Prologue

In a faraway land called Kaelumoor, where magic and science lived side by side, a dark prophecy loomed. Eight guardians were chosen to protect the Blue Rose, a special treasure that kept their world safe. But darkness crept in, turning the guardians against each other. Only Zina, the youngest, escaped with the Blue Rose.

She found herself on Earth, trapped inside a crystal, her memories fading. Centuries passed, but the darkness never gave up. Its followers, the seekers, searched tirelessly for the Blue Rose.

Then, in the bustling city of Gharana, a boy named KD accidentally stumbled upon Zina's prison. He didn't know it yet, but his life was about to change forever. He was about to become part of a battle bigger than anything he could have imagine.

I

The Forbidden Room

Life's a total drag. Exams are finally over, but I feel like a zombie who flunked the apocalypse. Meenal, the girl with eyes that could make the summer sky jealous, dumped me. Yeah, me, KD, the school's golden boy. More like tarnished brass these days.

Everything's gone all black and white, like someone spilled ink on my Technicolor world. It's been a week of moping around this creepy old house, drowning in boredom. The place is straight out of a horror movie, but without any of the cool special effects. Just endless shadows and dust bunnies. The only sounds are the creaking floorboards and the occasional hoot of an owl outside.

Speaking of shadows, they seem to have a life of their own here. They glide and crawl across the walls, lengthening and shortening as the sunlight shifts throughout the day. The old portraits lining the hallways watch me with stern expressions, their eyes seemingly following my every move. It's enough to give anyone the creeps.

My dad, the mad scientist, is no help. He's always locked away in his lab, muttering to himself and tinkering with strange contraptions. I swear I once heard him talking to a chair. He's brilliant, no doubt, but he's also completely oblivious to the fact that his only son is slowly turning into a human mold spore.

Desperate for something. Anything.. to break the monotony, I've resorted to exploring every nook and cranny of this dusty old mansion. There's got to be something interesting hidden away, right? I mean, this place is ancient. It practically screams secrets.

I started with the attic, a dark and musty space filled with cobwebs and forgotten relics. The air got the smell of mothballs and old paper. I sneezed so hard I thought my brain would rattle out of my ears, sending a cloud of dust swirling around me.

Rummaging through boxes, I unearthed a treasure trove of peculiar items: antique clothing that smelled of lavender and decay, stacks of letters tied with faded ribbons, and a collection of odd trinkets that could have been props from my dad's lab. A brass telescope, a tarnished monocle, and a jar filled with what looked like pickled eyeballs.

Then, a memory sparked. The forbidden room. The one my dad always warned me about, his voice dropping to a low growl: "Stay out of there, KD." But rules are like piñatas, meant to be broken open, right? I'm practically an adult now, eighteen in a few months. Time to see what Dad's been hiding.

I began my search for the key. My dad's study was a chaotic mess, a tornado of scientific papers and half-finished inventions. Wires snaked across the floor, and beakers filled with bubbling liquids perched precariously on shelves. I sifted through stacks of books, their titles ranging from "Advanced Astrophysics" to "The Necromancer's Cookbook."

Finally, tucked away in a hidden compartment beneath his desk, I found it. A small, tarnished key with an ornate handle. Jackpot.

With the key in hand, I made my way down the creaky hallway towards the forbidden room. The old floorboards groaned under my weight, like the house itself was trying to warn me away.

I reached the door, its dark wood etched with strange symbols I couldn't decipher. They resembled a mix of alchemical symbols and ancient runes, twisting and intertwining in a dizzying pattern. My heart pounded in my chest like a drum solo. I hesitated, a tide of doubt engulfed me

But curiosity, that relentless itch, won out.

I slid the key into the lock and turned it. I took a deep breath, pushed open the door, and stepped into the unknown.

My heart pounded like a tribal drumbeat as I crept towards the forbidden room, the old key heavy in my hand. The door, a slab of ancient, dark wood, groaned in protest as I turned the key and pushed it open.

A gust of stale, musty hit me as I stepped inside. The room was cloaked in darkness, a void that seemed to swallow the light. With trembling fingers, I flicked the switch, and the room blinked into a hazy existence.

It was like stumbling into another dimension. Shelves crammed with glass jars lined the walls, each filled with liquids of eerie greens and blues. Strange machines droned and stuttered, their lights casting an eerie glow over the room. Wires snaked across the floor, connecting everything to a central hub.. a massive, pulsating blue stone that dominated the center of the room.

The stone emanated a soft, ethereal light, as if it possessed a life of its own. It was mesmerizing, and I found myself drawn towards it. My hand reached out, hovering over its cool, smooth surface. A doubt settled over me. What if it was dangerous? What if it exploded?

But curiosity, that insatiable itch, urged me on. I closed my eyes and touched the stone. A jolt of energy surged through me, a tingling sensation that made the hairs on my arms stand on end. It wasn't painful, but it was... unsettling.

Suddenly, the room shuddered. The lights flickered and died, plunging me into darkness. My heart pounded in my chest like a trapped bird. The only illumination came from the blue stone, its glow now intensified, casting long shadows.

Then, a cracking sound. It was faint at first, but it grew louder, more insistent. The blue stone was fracturing, a spiderweb of cracks spreading across its surface. I held my breath, expecting an explosion, but what happened next was far stranger.

A blinding flash of light filled the room, so intense that I instinctively squeezed my eyes shut. When I cautiously opened them, the room was different. The air thrummed with an invisible energy, and the machines hummed with renewed vigor. But most astonishing of all, a figure now stood in the center of the room, where the blue stone had once been.

It was a woman, tall and slender. She was beautiful, but in a creepy kind of way. Her skin glowed, emanating a soft light that illuminated her features. She was emerging from the blue stone, slowly, like a flower blooming in time-lapse photography.

My jaw dropped. I blinked, thinking maybe I was hallucinating. I pinched myself. Ouch. Okay, I wasn't dreaming. The woman was real. She was coming out of the blue stone, her body materializing as if from thin air.

I was rooted to the spot, a mixture of awe and terror coursing through me. I blinked, thinking maybe I was hallucinating but the woman was real.

I felt like I was trapped in a scene from a sci-fi movie, but this was real life. And it was getting weirder by the second. I couldn't tear my eyes away. Her eyes, like pools of liquid moonlight, locked onto mine.

Every instinct screamed at me to run, to scream, to do something, anything! But my body was frozen, a statue sculpted from fear and disbelief. All I could do was stare, my mind racing to make sense of the impossible.

Was this a dream? A hallucination? Another pinch, another stab of pain. Definitely not a dream.

My brain felt like it was trying to download a terabyte of data in a nanosecond. A freaking alien had just materialized in my dad's lab. Or maybe she was a ghost, a demon, or something even crazier. The possibilities were endless, and each one more terrifying than the last.

Suddenly, she opened her mouth, and a stream of melodic sounds poured out. It wasn't any language I recognized, but it was strangely beautiful. I didn't understand a single word, but the melody seemed to resonate deep within me.

Fear and fascination warred within me, a turbulent storm raging in my chest. I tried to speak, to ask who she was and what she was doing here, but my voice was trapped in my throat. I couldn't speak.

Then, without warning, the melodic sounds shifted, morphing into words. Clear, crisp English words. "I am hungry," she said, her voice as smooth as velvet. A pause, then a surprising addition, "I need to clean myself."

I stood there, dumbfounded. She was hungry? Like, she needed to eat? And she wanted to clean herself? The absurdity of the situation threatened to overwhelm me.

She tilted her head, her luminous eyes searching mine. "I need to clean myself," she repeated, her voice gentle but insistent.

And then, without another word, she turned and glided towards the bathroom, her movements as graceful as a ballerina's. I watched, my jaw agape, as the bathroom door clicked shut behind her. The sound of running water filled the silence.

I stood outside the bathroom door, my mind reeling. What was she doing in there? Was she washing off stardust? Removing her exoskeleton? My imagination ran wild.

Finally, the water stopped. I heard the rustle of towels, then silence. A long, agonizing silence. Anxiety gnawed at me. Had she vanished?

❧

The door was finally open, and there she stood, wrapped in one of my dad's old, faded bathrobes. It was comically oversized, swamping her slender frame, but somehow, she made it look elegant. Her hair, damp and glistening, cascaded down her back like a waterfall of moonlight. She looked... human. Almost.

I was in shock. Like, major shock. A girl, or whatever she was, had just come out of my bathroom wearing my dad's bathrobe.

"I'm hungry" she repeated.

And now, she was hungry. I mean, I get hungry too, but this was different. This was an alien, or whatever she was.

I stumbled into the kitchen, my mind racing. What do you feed an alien? Pizza? Burgers? I didn't think so. I decided to go with something simple, something familiar, something human. I rummaged through the fridge. Bread, cheese, and some leftover tandoori chicken. Okay, this would have to do.

I started making sandwiches, my hands shaking slightly. Bread, cheese, chicken, a dollop of mint chutney for good measure. How hard could it be? I mean, I'm not exactly a Sanjeev Kapoor, but I can make a decent sandwich. I put the plates on the table, feeling a bit proud of myself. I hoped she liked sandwiches.

I went back to the living room and called her. "Food," I said, trying to sound casual, like this was just a normal Tuesday night. She looked at me, then at the kitchen, and then back at me. And then, she walked towards the kitchen, her bare feet silent on the cold tile floor.

I watched as she sat down at the table. Her eyes were on the sandwich, and for a moment, I thought she might explode or something. But then, she took a bite. Her eyes widened in surprise, and a subtle smile touched her lips. She took another bite, and then another, savoring each bite. I was starting to feel proud of myself.

She finished the sandwich in record time, every crumb disappearing as if by magic. "Good," she said, her voice still smooth and otherworldly. I nodded, feeling a strange sense of accomplishment.

Then, she looked at me directly, her eyes locking onto mine. "My name is Zina," she said. Just like that.. no explanation. Just, "My name is Zina."

I stared at her, my mind reeling. Zina. That was a weird name. And then it hit me. This wasn't a dream. This was real. A girl named Zina, who glowed, came out of a blue stone in my dad's lab, ate my sandwich, and introduced herself. My life officially sucked less. Or maybe, it was just getting started.

&

"Zina, huh?" I repeated, trying to sound cool. But inside, I was freaking out.

"Who are you exactly?" I managed to blurt out, my voice trembling slightly.

She looked at me, her eyes holding a universe of secrets. "I am Zina of Kaelumoor," she repeated, "One of the Eight Guardians. Trapped in the stone for centuries."

Eight what? I was lost. But I got the gist of it.

I tried to process what she had said. Eight? Guardians? Centuries? It was like trying to solve a complex math problem while being chased by a bear. My head was spinning.

"Kaelumoor?" I managed to squeak out. My voice sounded like a dying mouse.

She nodded, her expression calm, almost indifferent. "A realm of power and magic" she said, her voice like velvet.

I was starting to think that maybe I should invest in a good therapist.

I stared at her, my mind racing. Eight? What did that even mean? Guardians? Of what? The world? The galaxy?

She seemed to sense my confusion. "Guardians of balance," she said, her voice soft. "We are ancient beings, tasked with maintaining equilibrium in the universe."

Equilibrium? In my world? The world where people were more worried about their Instagram likes than world peace? I laughed, but it came out as a nervous chuckle. "You're kidding, right?"

She didn't laugh. Her expression was serious. "I am not," she replied.

I was starting to think I was losing my mind. I opened my mouth to say something, anything, but no words came out. I felt out of place.

"I'm... I'm KD," I finally managed to stutter out. "Kautilya D'Souza."

She nodded, her eyes studying me. "You are sad," she stated, her voice filled with a strange kind of understanding.

I was taken aback. How did she know I was sad? I mean, it was obvious, but still...

"Yeah, I guess I am," I mumbled, looking down at my hands.

"Why?"

The question caught me off guard. I hadn't really thought about it. I mean, I was sad because Meenal dumped me, and my dad was always away, and now there was this glowing woman in my kitchen. But how do you explain that to someone who probably lived for centuries?

"I don't know," I mumbled, looking down at my hands. "Just... life sucks, I guess."

She tilted her head, studying me. "Life is a cycle," she said, her voice filled with a wisdom that was both ancient and profound. "There is joy and sorrow, birth and death, light and darkness."

I blinked. She sounded like a philosopher or something. I was starting to think that maybe hanging out with aliens wasn't so bad after all.

She paused, as if considering something. Then, she said, "I thank you for freeing me. I owe you a debt."

I blinked. "Me? Free you?" I was confused. I hadn't done anything. It was the blue stone.

"Yes," she replied, her voice firm. "You broke the seal. You released me."

She paused again, her eyes scanning the room. "I must find the others," she said, her voice filled with a sense of urgency. "I need a place to stay while I search. Can I stay here, please?"

My mind was racing. She wanted to stay here? In my house? With me? This was insane. I mean, I was happy to have some company, but an alien? A supernatural being?

I opened my mouth to say something, but no words came out. I was too shocked. She just stood there, looking at me expectantly.

Finally, I managed to squeak out, "Uh, yeah, sure. I guess." I mean, what else was I supposed to say? Kick her out? That would be kind of heartless. And besides, she was kind of cool, in a terrifyingly alien way.

I gestured towards the guest room. "You can stay there," I said, trying to sound casual.

She nodded, her expression unchanged. Then, she turned and walked towards the guest room.

I watched her go, feeling a strange mix of fear and excitement. This was the craziest thing that had ever happened to me. I had to tell someone.

I grabbed my phone and started dialing. "Guys, you won't believe what just happened.."

II

Reality Check

The doorbell rang sharp, jolting me out of my daze.

Taking a deep breath, I opened the door to reveal Nooran and Mathew, my two best friends since childhood. They looked at me with a mix of curiosity and concern, their faces illuminated by the porch light.

"Dude, it's midnight," Mathew groaned, rubbing his eyes sleepily. "What's up?" Nooran chimed in, her voice laced with a hint of worry.

I didn't know how to start. How could I possibly explain the situation without sounding completely insane? I hesitated, the words caught in my throat.

"It's... it's weird," I finally managed to stammer out.

They exchanged a knowing glance. "Don't tell me you've seen a ghost again," Nooran joked, trying to lighten the mood.

I shook my head, unable to meet their eyes. This was far stranger than any ghost story.

"It's not a ghost," I said, my voice barely a whisper. "It's... something else."

Intrigued, they leaned in closer, their faces a mixture of skepticism and eager anticipation. I knew I had to tell them. It was too big a secret to bear alone.

"There's... there's a girl in my house," I blurted out, the words tumbling out in a rush.

Their eyes widened in disbelief. "What?" Mathew exclaimed, his voice rising an octave.

Nooran, always the practical one, interjected, "Slow down, KD. What do you mean, a girl? Like, a new girlfriend?"

I shook my head vehemently. "No, not like that. She's... different." I hesitated, searching for the right words. "She's not... human," I finally confessed, the words hanging heavy in the air.

They were stunned, their expressions a comical mix of shock and bewilderment. I knew they were expecting something weird, but this was beyond their wildest imagination.

"You're kidding, right?" Mathew finally managed to croak out, his voice thick with disbelief.

I shook my head again, a helpless gesture. "I wish I was," I replied, my voice barely a whisper.

Their expressions mirrored a kaleidoscope of emotions - shock, disbelief, a flicker of fear. I could almost hear the gears grinding in their brains, trying to reconcile this bizarre revelation with the friend they thought they knew.

Nooran, ever the leader, broke the silence. "Tell us everything," she commanded, her voice firm but laced with a tremor of anxiety.

I took a deep breath, steeling myself for the onslaught of questions. "Okay, but you have to promise not to freak out."

They nodded in unison, their eyes wide with a mix of apprehension and morbid curiosity.

With a hesitant step, I led them into the living room. Zina sat on the couch, an image of serene tranquility. She was wearing one of my dad's old, faded bathrobes, its hem pooling around her bare feet. Her hair, still slightly damp, cascaded down her back like a waterfall of moonlight. She looked like any other girl, if you ignored the faint, otherworldly glow that emanated from her skin.

"Guys, this is Zina," I announced, forcing a nonchalant tone into my voice.

Nooran and Mathew stared at her, their mouths agape like fish out of water. Zina offered a tentative smile, a small, almost shy gesture that seemed out of place on her otherworldly features.

"Hello," she greeted them softly, her voice barely a whisper.

They remained speechless, their eyes darting between me and Zina.

"She's... different," I offered lamely, hoping they would fill in the blanks.

Zina nodded in agreement. "I am," she confirmed simply, her eyes twinkling.

An uncomfortable silence descended upon the room. Mathew finally found his voice, "You're kidding, right?" he choked out, his gaze fixed on Zina.

I shook my head, unable to suppress a nervous chuckle.

Nooran looked like she was about to faint, her face pale and clammy.

I braced myself for the inevitable barrage of questions, the skepticism, the accusations of insanity. But before I could utter a word, Zina held out her hand, palm facing upwards. With a flick of her wrist, a crystal-clear glass materialized in her hand, filled to the brim with shimmering water. It was as if she had conjured it out of thin air.

Nooran and Mathew's eyes bulged, their jaws slack. They stared at the glass, then at Zina, then back at the glass again.

A slow grin spread across my face. I knew then that there was no going back. This was real. This was insane. And it was the most exciting thing that had ever happened to me.

And it was only the beginning.

The weirdest part was, I was starting to get used to it. Like, this was my life now. A life with an alien in my living room, who could conjure glasses of water out of thin air and speak in cryptic riddles. Cool. Totally cool.

No, wait, not cool. This is the worst. I need a vacation. From my life.

&

Nooran and Mathew were starting to look overwhelmed. I could see the fear and excitement battling it out in their eyes, like two wrestlers vying for the championship belt. I felt bad for them, dragging them into this mess, but at the same time, I was glad they were here. It was like having an audience to this crazy reality show called "My Life."

Finally, Nooran stood up, her legs wobbling slightly. "I think I need to go home and process this," she said, her voice shaky but resolute.

Mathew nodded, his face pale. "Yeah, me too," he mumbled, looking like he was about to hurl.

They both looked at me and Zina, then at each other. It was a silent agreement, a mutual understanding that this was too much to handle in one night.

"We'll call you," Nooran said, giving me a worried look, like I was a ticking time bomb about to explode.

I nodded, not trusting my voice. As they walked towards the door, I felt a pang of loneliness. They were my escape from this insane situation, my tether to normalcy, and now they were leaving.

The door closed, leaving me alone with Zina.

I turned to look at her. She was sitting on the couch, looking at the window. The city lights twinkled outside, their reflection in her luminous eyes. She looked almost ethereal, like a being from another world. Which, technically, she was.

But despite the fear and confusion swirling inside me, I also felt a strange sense of peace. With Zina around, I didn't feel as alone.

I was exhausted, my brain felt like a blender filled with too many thoughts. I needed sleep, a deep, dreamless slumber that would wash away the absurdity of the night. But how could I possibly sleep with all this going on? My mind was of too many questions, doubts, and a healthy dose of fear.

"I'm going to bed," I mumbled.

Zina nodded, her expression as serene as a Buddhist monk. "Rest," she said, her voice a gentle whisper.

I trudged to my room, my limbs heavy with exhaustion. As I closed the door, I glanced back at her. She was still sitting on the couch, the sight was both comforting and unsettling.

I flopped onto my bed, my body sinking into the familiar softness of the mattress. I stared at the ceiling, the shadows in the dim light. Aliens, guardians, magic, and me. It sounded like the premise of a bad comic book.

I tried to sleep, but my brain wouldn't shut off. It was like a hyperactive squirrel on a caffeine high, jumping from one thought to the next. Zina, her glowing eyes, the way she materialized out of thin air, the way she talked about balance and the universe as if they were old friends. It was all too much.

I checked the time on my phone. 1:00AM. Great. I had at least three more hours of this mental torture. I rolled over, burying my face in the pillow, hoping that sleep would claim me soon. But as the minutes ticked by, I realized that sleep was the last thing on my mind.

I was too wired, too excited, too terrified to even close my eyes. I knew this night would change my life forever. But how?

Only time would tell.

❧

Next morning, my head ached intensly. I opened my eyes slowly, the sunlight stabbing into my retinas like tiny daggers. As the fog of sleep cleared, the memories of last night flooded back.. the glowing stone, the ethereal woman, the mind-bending revelations.

As I walked out of my room and into the living room, I staggered so low it nearly hit the floor. The whole place was immaculate. Like, spotless. The couch cushions were plumped, the floor gleamed, and the windows sparkled as if they had been polished by a team of fairies. It looked like a scene from a cleaning product commercial.

I looked around, bewildered. Did a cleaning crew break in while I was sleeping? Did my dad finally snap and decide to embrace domesticity? No, neither seemed likely.

I looked at Zina, who was sitting on the couch, engrossed in a book titled "Quantum Physics for Dummies." She looked up, her eyes calm and serene, as if she had just spent the morning meditating in a Tibetan monastery.

"I cleaned," she said simply, her voice as smooth as honey.

I stared at her, dumbfounded. "You cleaned the whole house?" I asked, still struggling to grasp the concept.

She nodded, a small smile playing on her lips. "Efficiency is important," she replied, as if it were the most obvious thing in the world.

I just stood there, trying to process what she had done. She had cleaned the entire house in the time it took me to sleep. This girl was not only an alien, but she was also a super-efficient cleaning machine.

I needed coffee. Strong, black coffee.

Zina had made herself at home, spending most of her time in the living room, where she practiced a strange form of meditation. She would sit cross-legged on the floor, her eyes closed, her hands resting on her knees, a faint aura of energy surrounding her. Occasionally, I would catch her levitating objects – a spoon, a book, once even the family cat, Mr. Kumar, who looked absolutely terrified. Zina seemed oblivious to the chaos she was causing in my already chaotic life.

Despite the initial shock and confusion, we'd started to talk more, our conversations a strange blend of the mundane and the fantastical. She would tell me stories of her homeworld, Kaelumoor, a place filled with mythical creatures, ancient wisdom, and powerful magic. I, in turn, would share tales of Earth, our technological advancements, our political struggles, our obsession with social media.

It was like having a conversation with a time traveler from a distant future, or a wise sage from an ancient civilization. Zina possessed a vast knowledge of the universe, a deep understanding of the interconnectedness of all things. Her words often left me pondering the meaning of life, the universe, and everything in between.

The strangest part was, I was starting to get used to her presence. Zina was no longer a mysterious alien who had materialized out of a blue stone. She was just... Zina. A weird, quirky, otherworldly friend who happened to have a knack for cleaning and a penchant for levitating household objects.

She had become a part of my daily routine, a fixture in my life. It was as if she had always been there, a silent observer of my struggles and triumphs. And as the days passed, I realized that I didn't want her to leave. She was a part of my family now, a strange, unconventional, but undeniably important part.

☙

School was starting next week. The thought chilled me to the bone, a harsh reminder of reality crashing into my surreal summer. I was just getting used to this whole alien-in-my-living-room situation, the bizarre new normal that had become my life. And now I had to go back to the mundane world of bullies, boring teachers, and endless math equations.

With a sigh, I looked over at Zina, who was perched on the couch, engrossed in one of those ancient, leather-bound tomes she seemed to favor.

"School starts next week," I announced, trying to keep my voice casual, as if this weren't the most earth-shattering news of the century.

She looked up, her eyes filled with a curious light. "School," she repeated, rolling the word around in her mouth like a foreign delicacy.

"Yeah, school," I confirmed, feeling a bit foolish. "You know, where they teach you stuff?"

She nodded slowly, as if absorbing the concept. "You will return?" she asked, her voice laced with a hint of concern.

"Yeah, of course," I replied, surprised by her question. "I'll be back in the afternoons."

She simply nodded, her gaze returning to her book.

Going back to my room, a sense of dread settling over me. I couldn't believe I was actually going back to school after everything that had happened. It felt like a lifetime ago that I was just a normal teenager, dealing with normal teenage problems. Now, I had an alien living in my house, a secret that could change the world. How was I supposed to focus on algebra with that hanging over my head?

"Hey, Zina," I called out, pausing at my bedroom door. "Don't do anything crazy while I'm gone, okay?"

"I will remain here," she replied, her voice a soothing balm to my anxiety.

I nodded, feeling a kind of reassurance. At least I didn't have to worry about coming home to a house levitating in mid-air or a portal to another dimension in my backyard.

Or did I?

I shook my head, trying to banish the wild thoughts that threatened to consume me. I had a feeling this week was going to be a long one.

III

Guilty Until Proven Innocent

"Ughh man, I can't believe school is starting," I grumbled to myself, tossing a crumpled shirt onto the growing pile of clothes on my floor. It felt like just yesterday I was celebrating the end of exams, and now I was facing the grim reality of bullies, boring lectures, and the dreaded math tests. Great. Just great.

I was rummaging through my closet, trying to find a shirt that didn't look like it had been slept in for a week, when I heard a familiar honk outside. It was Mathew, my trusty sidekick in all things weird and wonderful.

I grabbed my backpack, which felt suspiciously light without the usual stack of textbooks, and headed out the door.

"Dude, you look like you haven't slept in days," Mathew commented as I slid into the passenger seat. He gave me a sideways glance, his eyebrows furrowed in concern.

"Thanks for the compliment," I retorted, my voice dripping with sarcasm. "I've been dealing with some crazy stuff, okay?"

We pulled out of the driveway, leaving the imposing silhouette of my house behind. I couldn't help but wonder what Zina was up to inside.

"So, the alien lady is still there?" Mathew asked, breaking the silence.

I sighed, a heavy weight settling on my chest. "She's still here, yeah," I corrected myself. "Zina. She's still here."

Mathew let out a low whistle. "Your life is officially weirder than mine," he declared, a hint of envy in his voice.

I shrugged, not knowing how to respond. What was there to say? My life had taken a sharp turn.. and I was just along for the ride.

We drove in silence for a few minutes, the only sound the hum of the engine and the occasional chirping of birds.

"So," Mathew began, his voice hesitant, "what's she like, really? I mean, besides the whole glowing and magical things?"

I pondered his question, trying to put into words the enigmatic being that was Zina. "She's... different," I finally said. "Really different. Like, she's calm and collected, but she's also incredibly powerful. And she knows everything."

Mathew's eyes widened. "Everything?"

I nodded solemnly. "Everything."

The rest of the drive to school was spent in silence, each of us lost in our own thoughts. As we pulled into the school parking lot, I looked back. It felt strange to be leaving Zina alone, like abandoning a child in a carnival.

I turned to Mathew, my voice barely above a whisper. "I'll tell you everything later," I promised.

He nodded, his face still carved with a mixture of fear and fascination.

We walked into the school, the familiar sights and a din of adolescent life swept over us. It was a world of lockers, gossip, and the constant drone of teachers lecturing. A normal world. A world without glowing aliens and weird stuff.

But as I entered my first-period class, the weight of Zina's presence settled back on my shoulders. I knew this was just a temporary reprieve, a brief respite from the extraordinary.

I found my seat and slumped down, my mind a jumble of equations and unanswered questions. I had to focus on school, on the mundane tasks that lay ahead. But all I could think about was Zina.

This was going to be a long day.

8○

Our first class was a snoozefest: some mandatory anti-drug campaign. Like, we get it, drugs are bad. We're not a bunch of brain-dead zombies. I was already bored out of my skull, my mind wandering back to Zina and her cryptic talk. I wondered what she'd make of this whole "Just Say No" propaganda. Probably find it as pointless as I did.

Staring out the window, I watched the clouds drift lazily across the sky, my thoughts a jumbled mess of aliens, magic, and high school drama. It was a bizarre combination, to say the least.

Suddenly, a familiar voice boomed through the classroom, jolting me out of my daydream. "Drugs are a poison to the soul" the voice declared, its tone a mix of authority and concern.

I turned around to see Officer Ravi, a local cop who had earned a reputation for being fair and understanding, standing at the front of the class. He was a towering figure, his uniform crisp and clean, his expression serious. A small smile tugged at my lips. At least this class wouldn't be a complete waste of time.

Officer Ravi launched into a lecture about the dangers of drug abuse, citing statistics, sharing personal anecdotes, and warning us about the consequences of addiction. I zoned out for a bit, my mind drifting back to Zina. I already knew drugs were bad. I just wanted to go home and pick her brain about interdimensional travel or something like that.

I looked Mathew, who was doodling Chutki on his notebook, his tongue sticking out in concentration. He looked as bored as I felt. We exchanged a knowing glance, a silent communication that said, "Can this class be over already?"

Despite the tedium of the lecture, I couldn't help but feel a sense of excitement bubbling beneath the surface. I had a secret, a mind-blowing secret that no one else knew. I had an alien living in my house, and she was teaching me about things that went far beyond the confines of this classroom.

I might be stuck in school, but my mind was already soaring through the cosmos.

The session was finally over. I stretched, my back cracking.

Mathew, slumped next to me, looked like he was ready to pass out.

"That was the longest forty-five minutes of my life," Mathew groaned, rubbing his temples.

I nodded in agreement. "Let's find Nooran," I suggested, eager to escape the stuffy classroom and get some fresh air.

We made our way through the crowded hallways, a bunch of students rushing to their next class. As we approached Nooran, I spotted her standing outside a classroom, chatting with a group of girls.

I felt relieved. Nooran was like a beacon of normalcy in this increasingly bizarre world. But as we drew closer, my stomach dropped.

Standing in the corridor, was Rohith. Meenal's new boyfriend. The guy was a grade-A jerk, a walking ego with a hair-trigger temper.

He spotted us and a smug smirk spread across his face. "Well, well, well," he drawled, his voice dripping with sarcasm. "If it isn't the loser duo. Back for another round of humiliation?"

Mathew tensed beside me, his fists clenching. I tried to ignore Rohith, but his words were like daggers, piercing my already bruised ego.

"You know, you should really give up on Meenal," Rohith continued, his voice rising. "She's way out of your league, dude. You're just a pathetic loser who can't move on. Face it, man, you'll never be good enough for her."

My blood boiled, a red-hot rage coursing through my veins. I took a step forward, my vision narrowing, my knuckles turning white.

"Shut up, Rohith," I growled, my voice low and dangerous.

He threw back his head and laughed, a harsh, mocking sound that grated on my nerves. "Or what, D'Souza? What are you gonna do?"

I couldn't take it anymore. The anger, the frustration, the weeks of pent-up emotions exploded inside me. Before I could think, my fist connected with his jaw, a satisfying crack resounding through the hallway.

A shocked silence fell over the crowd of students. Time seemed to slow down as Rohith stumbled backward, his eyes wide with surprise and pain. A trickle of blood seeped from the corner of his mouth.

I regretted it instantly. The sharp crack of bone on flesh, the shock in Rohith's eyes. I had crossed a line, a big one. I looked at Nooran and Mathew, their faces etched with a mix of shock and concern. I knew I was in deep trouble.

Rohith, clutching his bleeding nose, stared at me with a mixture of disbelief and fury. His posse, a pack of wannabe tough guys, circled around him, their eyes filled with a predatory gleam. This was bad, really bad.

"You're going to pay for this, D'Souza," Rohith snarled, his voice thick with venom.

I didn't bother to reply. There was nothing I could say that would undo the damage. I turned to Nooran and Mathew, my voice barely a whisper. "Let's go," I urged, my eyes darting nervously around the crowded hallway.

We beat a hasty retreat, the sound of Rohith's threats fading into the background as we hurried away.

We found a secluded spot beneath a sprawling banyan tree, its shade offering a temporary refuge from the chaos of the school. Nooran and Mathew stared at me, their eyes wide with a mixture of shock and disbelief.

"What was that about?" Nooran finally asked, her voice laced with a hint of accusation.

I shrugged, trying to feign nonchalance. "He was being a jerk," I replied, my voice a weak imitation of my usual swagger.

But deep down, I knew I had messed up. Big time. I had let my emotions get the better of me, and now I was paying the price.

We sat in silence for a few minutes. I could feel the tension hanging heavy around us.

⁊

The school bell broke the silence, signaling the start of our next class. We walked towards the building, our minds still reeling from the fight. I tried to focus on the teacher's droning voice, but my thoughts kept returning to Rohith's threat.

I was in trouble. Big trouble. I just hoped that he wouldn't press charges. But as I sat there, trying to look innocent, I saw a familiar figure standing at the classroom door. Inspector Desai, a stern-faced police officer, was staring directly at me, his arms crossed over his broad chest.

My heart sank. This was not going to end well.

My heart pounded like a war drum as Inspector Desai, known for his scrupulous odor, stood in our classroom, looked steadily at me. Heat flushed my face, and a cold sweat broke out on my palms. I was trapped in a spotlight, the target of a thousand accusing eyes.

Beside me, Mathew looked like he had seen a ghost, his eyes wide with terror. Nooran, usually the epitome of composure, was frozen in place, her mouth hanging open in shock.

Inspector Desai strode towards me, his face a mask of stone. "Kautilya D'Souza," he said, his voice low and ominous.

I managed a shaky nod, my voice barely audible. "Yes, sir."

He reached into his pocket and pulled out a small, clear plastic bag. Inside, a fine white powder glinted in the harsh fluorescent light. My stomach staggered as I recognized the telltale signs of illicit substances.

"This was found in your backpack," Inspector Desai said, his voice cold.

My mind went blank, a void of confusion and disbelief. Drugs? In my backpack? How? When? My gaze darted to Mathew and Nooran, their faces mirroring my own shock and bewilderment.

The realization hit me like a sledgehammer. I was being framed. Someone had planted those drugs in my backpack.

My life, already turned upside down by the arrival of Zina, was about to take another nosedive. This was worse than finding an alien in my living room. This was a nightmare, a cruel twist of fate that threatened to destroy my future.

Everything happened in a blur. One moment, I was a student, sitting in a classroom, listening to a lecture about the dangers of drugs. The next, I was a criminal, being handcuffed and escorted out of the school by a stern-faced police officer. The whispers and gasps of my classmates followed me like a swarm of angry bees.

Mathew and Nooran, my closest friends, looked at me with a mixture of shock and disbelief. Their eyes pleaded with me to explain, to deny the accusations, but I could only offer a helpless shrug. I tried to mouth the words "I didn't do it," but they were lost in the chaos.

৪৩

The walk to the police station felt like a death march. Each step was heavier than the last. I felt a profound sense of isolation, a loneliness that seeped into my very bones. I had no one to turn to, no one to believe in my innocence.

I was alone. Completely and utterly alone.

The police car's backseat was a cold, unforgiving cage. As we drove through the familiar streets, the city lights blurred into a phantasmagoria, a disorienting display that mirrored the turmoil in my mind. I felt like a character in a bad movie.

But this wasn't a movie. This was my life. And I was the main character, the one who was about to get screwed over. Hard.

Three hours. It felt like a lifetime. I had been confined to this cold, metal chair, my body aching from the rigid posture. The interrogation room was a confinement box, the walls closing in on me with every tick of the clock. The only light came from a single, flickering bulb that cast long, menacing shadows across the room.

The relentless questioning had left me feeling drained and defeated. Where did I get the drugs? Who gave them to me? Did I sell them to other students? The questions were like a broken record, repeating endlessly in my head. I had answered them truthfully, but my words fell on deaf ears. The police were convinced I was a delinquent, a drug dealer, a menace to society.

I stare at the clock on the wall, its hands moving at a glacial pace. It was already late afternoon, the golden sunlight streaming through the barred window a painful reminder of the freedom I had lost. I wondered where Mathew and Nooran were. Had they been questioned too? Were they worried sick about me?

A sense of despair defeated me. I was trapped, framed for a crime I didn't commit. The evidence was stacked against me, and I had no way to prove my innocence.

I buried my face in my hands, the cold metal of the handcuffs digging into my wrists. I was tired, scared, and utterly alone. All I wanted was to go home, to the familiar comfort of my bed, to the strange but reassuring presence of Zina.

Speaking of Zina, I wondered what she was doing. Was she aware of my situation? But how could she be? I was hoping she could do something to get me out. After all, she wasn't bound by the laws of this world.

But then, reality sunk in. Zina was just a girl, an alien girl. She might have extraordinary powers, but could she really fight against the authorities? Could she clear my name and prove my innocence?

I shook my head, trying to delete the doubts that plagued me. I had to focus on the present, on the immediate problem at hand. I had to find a way out of this mess, and I had to do it alone.

I was starting to lose hope. Despair gnawed at my inside, a growing pit of hopelessness. Maybe they were going to keep me here forever.

Just as I was about to give up, the door swung open with a bang. Inspector Desai strode in, his usually stoic face etched with a mixture of agitation and relief.

"You're free to go," he barked, his voice curt and clipped.

I stared at him, stunned. Free? Just like that? Was this some kind of cruel joke?

"But the drugs..." I stammered, my voice barely a whisper.

He cut me off, his eyes unwavering. "It was a mistake. You're free to go."

I was confused. One moment, I was a criminal, facing expulsion and a possible prison sentence. The next, I was innocent, cleared of all charges. It didn't make any sense.

As I was led out of the police station, my legs wobbling beneath me, I saw Mathew and Nooran waiting anxiously by the entrance. Their faces lit up when they saw me, their relief palpable.

We stepped out into the cool night air, the city lights a blur of color against the dark sky. The weight of the day's events pressed down on me, a heavy burden I couldn't shake off.

I knew this wasn't over. Someone had planted those drugs in my backpack, and they wouldn't give up so easily. A cold fury simmered beneath the surface of my confusion. I had a sinking feeling that Rohith was behind this, his smug face and venomous threats flashing through my mind.

Mathew and Nooran bombarded me with questions, their voices a jumble of concern and disbelief. I tried to explain, but the words wouldn't come. How could I explain something I didn't understand myself?

As we walked in silence, strange thoughts kept nagging at me.

Inspector Desai's voice interrupted my thoughts. "Hey, listen," he said, his tone softer now, almost apologetic. "Don't ask any questions. Just be grateful to Charlie."

Charlie, a name that sent chills down my spine. Gharana's most notorious crime lord, a murky figure who pulled the strings from behind the scenes. He saved me?

With that, he turned and disappeared into the night, leaving me standing there with Mathew and Nooran, the three of us united in our confusion and fear.

We walked home in silence. I had a feeling this was just the beginning of a much bigger storm, a storm that threatened to engulf us all. And at the center of it all, was Charlie.

បូ

I dragged myself through the front door, feeling like I had been run over by a steamroller. The emotional turmoil of the day had left me drained and exhausted. I collapsed onto the couch, my body sinking into the soft cushions with a sigh.

Zina was still perched on her usual spot, a worn leather-bound book open on her lap. She looked up as I entered, her eyes filled with a quiet understanding.

"A long day?" she inquired, her voice a soothing balm to my frayed nerves.

I nodded, unable to form words. A lump had formed in my throat, a knot of frustration and despair. She reached out, her slender fingers gently touching my shoulder. A warm, comforting energy flowed through me, easing the tension in my muscles.

I reached for my phone, my fingers fumbling as I dialed my dad's number. It rang a few times before he answered, his voice thick with sleep.

"Dad?" I croaked, my voice barely audible.

"KD, is everything okay?" he asked, his tone instantly alert.

"It's a long story," I replied, trying to maintain composure. "Can we talk later?"

He agreed, his voice heavy with concern. We hung up, and I sat there, staring blankly at the wall, my mind a jumble of thoughts and emotions.

But the questions wouldn't leave me alone. I had to know more.

I dialed my dad's number again, my heart pounded with intensity. This time, I wouldn't hold back.

"Dad," I began, my voice trembling slightly. "Do you know a man named Charlie?"

A long silence stretched between us, thick with unspoken tension. "Why do you ask?" he finally replied, his voice cautious, guarded.

"It's a long story," I said, my grip tightening on the phone. "But I think he's involved in something big, something dangerous."

Another pause, pregnant with meaning. Then, my dad uttered the words that would change everything. "I used to work for his father," he confessed, his voice heavy with regret.

The revelation hit me like a lightning bolt, electrifying every nerve in my body. My dad had worked for Charlie's father? The pieces of the puzzle were starting to fit together, but the picture they formed was a dark and disturbing one.

I knew I had to find out more, to uncover the secrets that my dad had kept hidden for so long. But for now, I just needed to sleep. I needed to escape, if only for a few hours, from the chaos that had become my life.

I closed my eyes, willing myself to drift away.

IV
Face-off

My mind was a storm of thoughts, each one more confusing than the last. Why would Charlie, the city's most notorious crime lord, stick his neck out for me, a nobody high school kid? It didn't make any sense. The guy was a ruthless predator, a shark who wouldn't hesitate to devour anyone who crossed his path. So, why me?

I tossed and turned in bed, the sheets tangled around my legs like a straitjacket. Sleep was a distant dream, a luxury I couldn't afford in this state of agitated confusion. I reached for my phone, searching for any information about Charlie, any clue that could shed light on his motives.

But the internet was a barren wasteland, offering nothing but recycled news articles about his criminal empire. It was like trying to find a grain of sand in the Sahara desert. Frustration gnawed at me, a bitter taste in my mouth.

I threw the phone aside and stumbled out of bed, my limbs heavy with exhaustion. I made my way to the kitchen, the floorboards creaking beneath my bare feet. I filled a glass with water.

Zina was in the living room, her eyes closed, her body perfectly still. A faint aura of light surrounded her, like a halo. I hesitated, not wanting to disturb her meditation, but the questions swirling in my mind demanded answers.

"Zina," I whispered, my voice barely audible in the silent house.

Her eyes snapped open, her gaze piercing through me. "You seem troubled," she observed.

I nodded, unable to meet her gaze. "I can't figure out why Charlie would protect me," I confessed, the words heavy with shame.

She listened patiently, her otherworldly eyes never leaving mine. "Perhaps his motives are unknown to you," she finally said, her voice a gentle caress. "Or perhaps," she added, "there is more to this situation than meets the eye."

"Great," I muttered sarcastically. "That was helpful." I nodded, my head feeling like it was stuffed with cotton wool.

Zina's cryptic words did little to ease my confusion. She was like a walking riddle, speaking in half-truths and cryptic prophecies. I wanted answers, not riddles. But I knew that Zina operated on a different level, a plane of existence where logic and reason didn't always apply.

After a moment of silence, she spoke again, her voice filled with a quiet determination. "I am searching for my home, Kaelumoor," she said, her eyes flickering with a longing I couldn't quite comprehend. "But I will watch over you. If you need assistance, do not hesitate to ask."

I appreciated the offer, but a stubborn pride rose within me. "It's my mess, Zina," I said, my voice firmer than I intended. "I'll sort it out."

She nodded, her expression a mask of acceptance. "As you wish," she replied.

I turned and went back to my room, leaving her to her meditation.

I would find out why he had helped me, and I would clear my name. This was my fight, and I would see it through to the end.

୫

The next morning, fueled by a potent mix of adrenaline and caffeine, I decided to confront Rohith head-on. It was a risky move, like poking a sleeping tiger with a stick, but I had to know the truth.

I found him in the cafeteria, surrounded by his usual entourage of sycophants. They were laughing loudly, their voices echoing through the crowded space. Rohith, with his perfectly styled hair and arrogant smirk, looked like he owned the place.

I marched up to him, ignoring the snickers and whispers that followed me. He looked surprised to see me, his smirk faltering for a moment.

I cut to the chase, my voice low and steady. "I need to talk to you," I said, my eyes boring into his.

He raised an eyebrow, clearly enjoying the attention. "Oh really?" he said, leaning back in his chair. "And what's this all about?"

I took a deep breath, trying to control the anger bubbling beneath the surface. "About the other day," I said, "The drugs."

His smirk disappeared, replaced by a flicker of fear that he quickly masked with a sneer. "What about it?" he challenged, trying to sound tough.

"I know it was you," I said, my gaze unwavering.

His face flushed with anger, his eyes narrowed into slits. "What the hell are you talking about?" he shouted, his voice rising above the din of the cafeteria.

I ignored his theatrics. "I want to know why," I said, my voice calm but resolute. "And I want to know about Charlie."

The mention of Charlie's name seemed to hit a nerve. His eyes narrowed further, and his jaw tightened. "Charlie? What's he got to do with anything?"

"I think he's mixed up in this," I said, my voice unwavering.

He burst out laughing, but the sound was hollow, forced. "You're losing it, man," he sneered. "Charlie? That's a joke, right?"

I didn't answer. I just stared at him, a silent challenge.

After a long, tense moment, Rohith finally broke the silence. "If you think you're so smart," he hissed, his voice barely audible, "figure it out yourself."

With that, he stood up abruptly, knocking over his chair, and stormed out of the cafeteria, his cronies scrambling to follow.

With that, Rohith and his cronies vanished, leaving me standing alone, my mind a maelstrom of anger and confusion. I had hoped for answers, for a confession, for some kind of resolution. But all I got was a cryptic warning and a glimpse of fear in Rohith's eyes.

I clenched my fists, the anger bubbling inside me threatening to boil over. But I took a deep breath, forcing myself to calm down. This wasn't the time for emotional outbursts. This was the time for action.

જી

I tracked down Mathew at the basketball court, his usual hangout after school. He was shooting hoops, his movements fluid and effortless. He looked surprised to see me, a flicker of concern crossing his face.

"Hey man, what's going on?" he asked, bouncing the ball in a pattern.

I didn't waste any time on pleasantries. "I need your help," I said, my voice tight with urgency.

He stopped dribbling, the ball falling to the ground with a dull thud. "With what?" he asked, his eyes narrowing.

"I need to find Charlie," I said, meeting his gaze with unwavering determination.

His face paled, his eyes widening in alarm. "Dude, are you nuts? That guy's dangerous! You don't want to mess with him."

I knew he was right, but I couldn't just sit back and do nothing. "I know it's risky," I said.. "But I have to try. I have to know what he's up to."

We slumped onto the weathered wooden bench. The setting sun cast long shadows across the court, painting a picture of impending doom. We were two teenagers, armed with nothing but our wits and a burning desire for justice. We had no idea what we were getting ourselves into, but we both knew one thing: we had to do this.

For me, it was about proving my innocence, and exposing the real culprit. For Mathew, it was about loyalty, about standing by his friend through thick and thin.

༄

We holed up in my room for the next few days, transforming it into a makeshift detective agency. Laptops droned and papers rustled. Mathew, the tech wizard of our duo, worked his magic on the internet, digging up dirt on Charlie and his empire.

It was like peeling an onion, layer after layer revealing a more pungent stench of corruption. We uncovered a labyrinth of shady dealings, illegal activities that ranged from drug smuggling to human trafficking. Charlie wasn't just a crime lord; he was a cancer, a parasite feeding on the misery of others.

As we delved deeper into Charlie's world, a sense of dread settled over us. This was bigger than we had ever imagined. We were playing a dangerous game, and the stakes were higher than we had ever dared to dream.

While Mathew was hunched over his laptop, sniffing out every scrap of information on Charlie, I found myself drawn to Zina. She was a constant presence in the living room, a silent observer of our frantic investigations. Her calm demeanor and enigmatic aura both fascinated and unnerved me.

I settled onto the couch beside her, my eyes drawn to the ancient tome she held in her delicate hands. The pages were filled with strange symbols and faded script, a language that seemed to whisper secrets from another world.

"You're working hard," she noticed.

"I'm still trying to figure out why Charlie would protect me," I confessed, my voice heavy with frustration.

She listened patiently, with an understanding that transcended words. "Perhaps there is a connection you are unaware of," she suggested.

Could there be a hidden link between me and Charlie, a connection that I hadn't even considered?

Nooran joined us, her face etched with exhaustion but her eyes burning with determination. "I've been talking to some people," she announced.. "There are rumors about Charlie having connections in high places. Politicians, judges, even some cops."

We exchanged glances, a silent acknowledgment of the gravity of her words. The scope of Charlie's influence was far greater than we had ever imagined. We were up against a powerful enemy, one who could easily crush us if we weren't careful.

Despair hit me, threatening to drown me in its icy grip. We were outmatched, outgunned, out of our depth. This was a battle we couldn't win.

As the days bled into nights, our quest for answers became an obsession.

Mathew's eyes were bloodshot, his fingers twitching with nervous energy. Nooran's usually cheerful demeanor had given way to a grim determination. They had pushed themselves to the limit, their minds and bodies exhausted from the relentless pursuit of information.

"We need to rest," Nooran declared, her voice hoarse from lack of sleep. "We're not going to accomplish anything if we collapse."

Mathew nodded in agreement, his shoulders slumped with fatigue. "We'll come back tomorrow," he promised, his voice barely above a whisper. "With fresh eyes and a clear head."

I watched them leave, their footsteps echoing in the empty hall. A wave of loneliness was what I felt next, the silence of the house amplifying my anxieties. I turned to Zina, her looks fixed on the flames in the fireplace. Her expression was unreadable.

"They need rest," she said softly, her voice a soothing balm to my frayed nerves.

I nodded, my throat tight with unspoken worry. "I know," I whispered.

I was alone now, alone with my thoughts and the looming threat of Charlie's unknown motives. The house groaned around me, the shadows seeming to grow longer and darker with each passing minute.

Then, Zina's voice, calm and measured, cut through the silence. "Perhaps it is time to take a more direct approach."

I looked at her, startled by her sudden suggestion. "What do you mean?" I asked, my voice barely above a whisper.

"We could seek out Charlie," she said.

I was taken aback. "Are you serious?" I exclaimed, my voice rising an octave. "That's incredibly dangerous! He's a ruthless criminal, Zina. He wouldn't hesitate to..." I trailed off, unable to finish the sentence.

She nodded, her expression serene. "I am aware of the risks," she said. "But it may be the only way to get the answers you seek."

I hesitated, torn between the desire for knowledge and the fear of the unknown. The clock ticked relentlessly, each second a reminder of the time slipping through my fingers.

A surge of adrenaline coursed through me, a spark of defiance igniting in my chest. I had been running from my problems for too long. It was time to face them head-on.

"Let's do it," I declared, my voice steady.

As darkness fell, we ventured into the Gharana City. The once familiar streets had transformed into a menacing labyrinth, the shadows deeper, the neon signs casting an eerie glow over the grimy sidewalks. The air was thick with the stench of stale urine and rotting garbage, a putrid symphony of urban decay.

The city's underbelly pulsed with a hidden life, a world of secrets and danger that most people were blissfully unaware of. Figures emerged from the shadows, their faces etched with desperation and despair. It was a world where survival was the only law, where trust was a currency rarely traded.

As we walked, I couldn't shake the feeling that we were being watched, that unseen eyes followed our every move. A cold shiver ran down my spine. This was a different world, a world where the line between good and evil was blurred, where the rules were different, and the consequences were dire.

We walked for what felt like an eternity, the city's nocturnal creatures watching us with curious eyes. A knot of tension tightened in my stomach, a mixture of fear and anticipation.

Just as I was about to give up hope, Zina stopped abruptly, her hand reaching out to halt my progress.

"There," she said, pointing to a dimly lit building across the street.

I squinted, trying to make out the structure in the darkness. It was an abandoned warehouse, its brick facade scarred by years of neglect and decay. The windows were boarded up, and the only light came from a single, flickering bulb hanging precariously above the entrance.

"Are you sure?" I asked, doubt creeping into my voice.

Zina nodded, her expression resolute. We exchanged a glance, a silent understanding passing between us. Without a word, we crossed the street, our footsteps echoing in the deserted alleyway.

This was it. The moment of truth.

The warehouse loomed ahead, a shadowy monster against the night sky. It looked like the perfect setting for a horror movie, the kind where unsuspecting teenagers wander into a dark and sinister place, never to be seen again. My heart pounded in unison as we approached.

We stepped inside the warehouse, the heavy metal door groaning in protest. The air was heavy with the smell of dust and mildew, and a faint metallic tang that sent a shiver down my spine.

We moved cautiously, our senses on high alert. The silence was deafening, broken only by the occasional creak of the old floorboards beneath our feet. Suddenly, a light turned on, revealing a cavernous space filled with shadows. Men lurked in the corners, their faces hidden in the dim light. They were large, muscular figures, their bodies tense, their hands hovering near unseen weapons.

This was it. The moment we'd been dreading. The men turned to face us, their eyes narrowed with suspicion. One of them, a behemoth with a shaved head and a scar that ran from his temple to his chin, stepped forward. "What do you want?" he growled, his voice rough and menacing.

I swallowed hard, my throat dry as sandpaper. "I want to talk to Charlie," I said, trying to project an air of confidence I didn't feel.

The big guy let out a harsh bark of laughter. "You must be lost, kid," he sneered. "This ain't no daycare center."

Zina stepped forward, her voice surprisingly calm in the face of danger. "We know why you're here," she said, her eyes meeting his without flinching. "We just want to talk."

The men exchanged uneasy glances, their postures shifting slightly. The big guy opened his mouth to speak, but I cut him off.

"Charlie protected me," I said, my voice unwavering. "I want to know why."

A hush fell over the room, the silence broken only by the distant drip of water from a leaky pipe. The men looked at each other, then back at us, their expressions a mix of confusion and curiosity. The big guy took a menacing step forward, his bulk casting a long shadow over us.

"Kid, you're way out of your league," he warned, his voice low and threatening.

I held my ground, my gaze locked with his. "I need to talk to him," I repeated, my voice firm.

A tense silence hung, heavy with the weight of unspoken threats. The men exchanged furtive glances, a silent conversation playing out in their eyes. It felt like an eternity before the big guy finally nodded, a reluctant acquiescence to our demands.

"Fine," he grunted, his voice laced with a thick layer of sarcasm. He jerked his thumb towards a heavy metal door at the far end of the warehouse. "Go on."

Zina and I exchanged a quick glance, a silent acknowledgement of the danger we were walking into. This could easily be a trap, a ploy to lure us into a false sense of security before they pounced. But we had come too far to turn back now. With a deep breath, we walked towards the door.

Before we could reach our destination, two more men stepped out of the shadows, blocking our path. They were lean and wiry, their faces hardened by a life of crime. They sized us up with cold, calculating eyes, their hands patting us down for weapons.

After what felt like an eternity, they nodded to each other, a silent signal that we were clear. They stepped aside, their eyes never leaving us as we continued down the long, dimly lit corridor. The walls were bare, the only decoration a series of ominous stains that hinted at a violent past.

At the end of the corridor, a heavy metal door stood sentinel, its surface scarred and dented. It slid open with a hiss, revealing a small, sparsely furnished room.

We stepped inside, the door closing behind us.

The room felt like a cage, the walls closing in on us with each passing second.

Minutes dragged by, each one stretching into an agonizing eternity. Just as I was about to crack, the door came open, and a figure emerged from the darkness.

❧

A woman stepped into the room, her presence commanding the space like a queen surveying her court. She was breathtaking, her beauty a blend of the exotic and the ethereal. Her eyes, the color of storm clouds, held a depth of mystery that both intrigued and intimidated. She looked barely older than me, yet there was a wisdom in her looks.

"Nice to finally meet you, kid," she said, her voice as smooth as velvet, a stark contrast to the harsh surroundings.

I was speechless, my mind reeling. Charlie? A woman? And so young? The realization hit me like a bucket of ice water. This was the infamous Charlie, the mastermind behind the city's criminal underworld.

Her look shifted to Zina, a playful glint in her eyes. "And you must be his girlfriend?" she inquired, her tone laced with a hint of amusement. "You look a bit older than him, don't you think?"

Zina's expression remained unchanged, her voice calm and measured. "No, I am not his girlfriend. My name is Zina.. and yes, I am older than him."

The woman turned back to me, her smile widening. "So," she said, her voice dripping with honeyed malice, "you wanted to talk."

I nodded, my throat dry, my mind racing to catch up with the reality of the situation. "Why did you protect me?" I blurted out, the question tumbling from my lips before I could stop it.

Her smile widened, a knowing curve that sent chills down my spine. "Your father worked for mine," she revealed, her voice a caress of velvet over steel. "An old debt, you see."

A cold dread settled in the pit of my stomach. This couldn't be the whole story. There was something more, something lurking beneath the surface, something she wasn't telling me.

"Just a debt?" I pressed.

She paused, her dark eyes boring into mine, searching for something I couldn't fathom. "For now," she finally replied.

I knew there was more to this, a hidden agenda, a secret motive that she wasn't willing to reveal. And I was determined to uncover it, no matter the cost.

The woman, the enigmatic Charlie, leaned back in her chair, a predatory smile playing on her lips. "You're a curious one, aren't you, KD?" she purred, her voice a silken trap. "But curiosity can be a dangerous thing, especially in this world."

A heavy silence descended upon the room.

Suddenly, Charlie's demeanor shifted. The playful facade vanished, replaced by a steely resolve. "You need to leave," she said abruptly, her voice laced with a hint of urgency.

We were taken aback, our confusion evident on our faces. "What?" I managed to stammer out, my voice thick with disbelief.

"It's not safe for you here," she explained, her tone brooking no argument. "They'll be after you."

Zina nodded in agreement.

The moment we had stepped into this warehouse, we had crossed a line, entered a world where danger lurked around every corner.

"But..." I began, a protest forming on my lips.

She cut me off, her voice firm. "Trust me," she said. "I'll take care of things."

There was a finality to her tone, a command that left no room for debate. We knew she was right. We had to go, to disappear back into the shadows.

We turned to leave,

I couldn't shake the feeling that we were leaving more questions than answers behind.

But one thing was certain: my life has irrevocably changed.

V
Superhero!

"Hey, Zina," I said one morning, trying to sound nonchalant even though my heart was doing a frantic tap dance. "Wanna see the sights?"

She looked up from her ancient tome, her eyes sparkling with curiosity. "Sights?" she asked.

"Yeah, you know, the cool stuff around here," I explained, gesturing vaguely towards the window. "Malls, parks, maybe even a street food stall if you're feeling adventurous."

"I would like that," she said, with a rare smile on her face.

Score! Maybe this wouldn't be a complete disaster after all.

Our first stop was the local mall, a sprawling behemoth of consumerism. Zina seemed mesmerized by the sheer scale of it all, her eyes wide with wonder as we navigated the maze of shops and escalators. She marveled at the flashing neon signs, the endless rows of clothes, the cacophony of sounds and smells. At one point, she even tried on a pair of oversized sunglasses, a mischievous grin spreading across her face. Who knew aliens could rock shades?

Next, we ventured into the city park, a green oasis amidst the concrete jungle. Children squealed with delight as they chased each other across the playground, their laughter a welcome contrast to the city's usual soundtrack of honking horns and blaring sirens. Zina watched them, a wistful expression softening her features.

"They seem happy," she observed.

"Yeah," I agreed, a pang of nostalgia tugging at my heart. "Kids are usually pretty carefree."

We spent hours in the park, sitting on a bench beneath a sprawling banyan tree, watching the world go by. It was a simple pleasure, a slice of normalcy in a life that had become anything but normal.

As we were leaving, the serenity was shattered by a scene ripped straight from a Bollywood movie.

A bank robbery was happening before our very eyes. Masked men, their faces obscured by black balaclavas, burst out of the bank, their arms laden with bulging bags of cash. Screams erupted from the crowd as people scattered in panic, seeking cover from the unfolding chaos.

But Zina didn't hesitate. With a grace that belied her otherworldly origins, she stepped forward towards the robbers, her eyes glowing with an eerie, pulsating light. I watched, mesmerized, as she raised her hand, a silent command hanging in the air.

Suddenly, the robbers froze, their bodies contorted in unnatural positions, as if an invisible force had seized control of them. The bags of cash slipped from their grasp, tumbling onto the pavement with a dull thud. They stumbled and fell, their movements jerky and uncoordinated, their cries of surprise muffled by their masks.

It was over in a matter of seconds. The robbers lay sprawled on the ground, incapacitated, their ill-gotten gains scattered around them. The crowd, moments ago a scene of panic, now stood in stunned silence, their eyes fixed on Zina. She turned to me, her eyes returning to their normal, mesmerizing blue.

"We should go," she said, her voice calm and unruffled.

I nodded, my mind still reeling from the display of power I had just witnessed. We slipped away into the crowd, two shadows disappearing into the twilight. As we walked, the sirens wailed in the distance, a reminder of the chaos we had left behind.

I looked at Zina, my heart filled with a mixture of awe and fear. She was more than just an alien, more than just a guardian. She was a force to be reckoned with, a power that could shape the world around her. And I was caught in her orbit, a passenger on a journey that was only just beginning.

As we walked back to the mansion with a sense of exhaustion from the day's events, the adrenaline had faded, replaced by a lingering sense of awe and apprehension.

But as I looked at Zina, a new worry crept into my mind. If she could effortlessly subdue those hardened criminals, what else was she capable of? Was she a benevolent force, or could she just as easily turn her power against us?

℘

News of Zina's intervention at the bank robbery spread like wildfire through the city's criminal underworld. The grapevine, always buzzing with rumors and whispers, carried the tale of the mysterious woman who had single-handedly thwarted a heist. Word reached Charlie's ears, and she knew that Zina was more than just a pretty face.

A few days later, a sleek black car pulled up to the mansion, its tires crunching on the gravel driveway. My heart sank as I recognized Charlie stepping out, her presence as imposing as ever. She was dressed in a tailored black suit, every inch the powerful businesswoman. But beneath the polished exterior, I could sense a dangerous predator, a coiled serpent ready to strike.

I met her at the door, forcing a smile onto my face despite the knot of anxiety in my stomach. "Hello, KD," she purred, her voice a seductive whisper. "I hope you're treating Zina well."

"Of course," I stammered, my voice betraying my nervousness.

She swept past me, her gaze sweeping over the room until it landed on Zina, who was sitting on the couch, engrossed in her book. A tense silence fell over the room.

"Zina," Charlie said, her voice as sharp as a knife. "We need to talk."

Zina closed her book, her eyes meeting Charlie's with an unwavering calm that belied the tension in the room.

"I hear you've been causing some trouble," Charlie continued, her voice dripping with menace. "Interfering in matters that don't concern you."

A surge of anger coursed through me. How dare she threaten Zina in my own home? But before I could voice my protest, Zina spoke.

"I was merely protecting the innocent," she said, her voice as smooth as silk, yet firm as steel.

Charlie let out a harsh, humorless laugh. "Innocent? Those were my men, Zina. My people."

"They were harming others," Zina replied, her voice unwavering. "I could not stand idly by."

Charlie leaned forward, her eyes narrowing into predatory slits. "I don't appreciate interference," she hissed, her voice laced with barely contained fury. "Consider this a warning, Zina. Stay out of my affairs."

Taking a deep breath, I stepped forward, placing myself between Zina and Charlie. "Don't worry, Charlie," I said, my voice surprisingly steady despite the turmoil inside me. "Zina won't cause any more trouble."

Charlie's gaze shifted to me, a cruel smirk twisting her lips. "Good," she said, her voice dripping with condescension.

With a final, lingering look at Zina, she turned and walked out, the door clicking shut behind her. The silence that followed was deafening, the tension in the room still palpable.

I turned to Zina, my heart pounding in my chest. "Are you okay?" I asked, my voice filled with genuine concern.

She met my gaze, a small smile gracing her lips. "I am fine." she reassured me. "Do not worry about me."

I nodded, but the worry didn't dissipate. Charlie's threat hung heavy.

We were caught in a dangerous game, and the stakes had just been raised.

I knew Zina possessed powers beyond my comprehension. Her display of strength during the bank robbery had been a stark reminder of her otherworldly abilities. But even with her formidable skills, I couldn't shake the gnawing worry that Charlie's threat was more than just empty words. She was a dangerous adversary, a predator lurking in the shadows, waiting for the perfect moment to strike.

&

The encounter with Charlie left a bitter taste in my mouth, a lingering unease that refused to dissipate. It wasn't just her veiled threats; it was the mystery surrounding my dad's past, the secrets he had kept hidden for so long. Why had he worked for Charlie's father? What dark secrets did he harbor? The questions gnawed at me, demanding answers.

"Zina," I said, my voice filled with a renewed sense of purpose. "We need to search the house."

She looked at me, her eyes mirroring my resolve. "What are we looking for?"

"Anything," I replied, my voice a low growl. "Records, documents, anything that could shed light on my dad's connection to Charlie's father."

She nodded, "Let us begin."

With Zina's help, the search was surprisingly efficient. Her supernatural speed and keen senses allowed us to scour the entire mansion in a matter of hours. We delved into dusty attics, explored forgotten basements, and even discovered a hidden compartment behind a loose brick in the library.

Amongst the piles of old records and faded photographs, we found several pictures of Charlie's father. His cold, calculating eyes seemed to pierce through the paper, a chilling reminder of the man's ruthless nature.

But the most disturbing discovery was a contract bearing my dad's signature. It detailed the construction of a state-of-the-art laboratory, equipped to handle highly dangerous and volatile chemicals. Curiosity piqued, I went online and researched the chemicals listed in the contract. My blood ran cold as I realized their destructive potential. These chemicals, if combined in the wrong way, could level an entire city block.

What had my dad been involved in? Why would he build a lab capable of such devastation? And what role did Charlie's father play in all of this?

I looked at Zina, my mind reeling. "This doesn't make any sense," I whispered, my voice choked with emotion.

She placed a comforting hand on my shoulder, her touch a warm anchor in the storm of my confusion. "Patience," she said softly. "The truth will reveal itself in time."

I nodded, trying to suppress the knot of fear that tightened in my stomach. Zina's words offered little comfort. The weight of the unknown, the looming threat of Charlie's power, and the unsettling revelations about my father's past left me feeling overwhelmed. This was bigger than I ever imagined, a tangled web of secrets and danger that threatened to consume me.

As Zina continued her relentless search, her sharp eyes fell upon a worn, leather-bound book tucked away in a hidden alcove in the library. The title, embossed in faded gold lettering, read Kaelumoor: The Guardian's World, authored by none other than Dr. Kael D'Souza - my dad.

My heart skipped a beat.

With her supernatural abilities, Zina devoured the book at an astonishing pace, her eyes scanning the pages with lightning speed. I watched, mesmerized, as her expression shifted from curiosity to sadness, then to a deep, heart-wrenching sorrow. Tears welled up in her eyes, shimmering like diamonds in the dim light.

Suddenly, a surge of energy crackled around her, the air charged with an otherworldly power. The book in her hands burst into flames, the pages curling and blackening in an instant. I gasped in shock, the sudden heat scorching my face.

"Zina! What did you do?" I exclaimed, my voice filled with disbelief and anger.

She looked at me, her eyes glistening with unshed tears. "It was necessary," she said, her voice barely a whisper.

"Necessary?" I retorted, my voice rising in anger. "That was my dad's book! Why would you destroy it?"

She remained silent, her gaze fixed on the smoldering remains of the book. The room filled with the acrid smell of burnt paper, a poignant reminder of the knowledge that had been lost.

"You have no right," I continued, my voice shaking with rage. "That was the only link I had to my dad's past, to understanding who he really was."

For the first time since I met her, Zina looked vulnerable. Her shoulders slumped, and a single tear rolled down her cheek, leaving a shimmering trail on her flawless skin.

"I am sorry" she whispered, her voice choked with emotion. "But it was for the best."

I stared at her, my anger slowly dissipating, replaced by a cold, unsettling curiosity. What secrets did that book hold? What had Zina seen that had compelled her to destroy it?

The questions swirled in my mind, a tempest of confusion and fear. But one thing was certain: the truth, whatever it might be, was far more dangerous than I could have ever imagined.

The questions swirled in my mind, a relentless storm of curiosity and doubt. Why would she destroy the book? What secrets did it hold? And how did it connect her to my father and Charlie?

I reached out instinctively, my hand hovering over her arm, a silent plea for comfort and understanding. But she flinched, her eyes widening with a pain that pierced my heart.

"I must go," she whispered, her voice brittle, her usual composure shattered. "I need to be alone."

She turned and fled the room, leaving me standing in the silent aftermath. A sense of betrayal gnawed at me, a bitter aftertaste to the burning questions that remained unanswered.

&

Days turned into nights, and Zina became a ghost haunting the halls of the mansion. The usual calm and serenity that surrounded her had been replaced by a melancholic silence. She retreated into her own world, spending hours meditating in her room, her eyes closed, her expression unreadable.

I tried to reach out to her, to offer comfort and support, but she remained distant, a fortress of impenetrable walls. The once vibrant connection we shared seemed to have faded, replaced by an awkward silence.

One morning, as I was nursing a cup of coffee and contemplating the mysteries that surrounded us, Zina surprised me. "KD," she said, her voice soft and hesitant. "Would you like to take a walk in the park?"

I looked up, startled by her sudden request. It was the first time she had initiated any kind of outing since the incident in the library. "Sure," I replied. Maybe this was a sign that she was ready to open up, to share the burden she carried.

We walked in silence for a while, the crisp autumn air swirling around us, carrying the scent of fallen leaves and damp earth. The park was alive with activity, children's laughter echoing through the trees, couples strolling hand-in-hand along the winding paths.

Zina's gaze lingered on a group of children playing tag, their faces alight with joy and carefree abandon. A wistful expression crossed her features, a longing for a simpler time, a world untouched by darkness and deceit.

Suddenly, a woman's panicked scream shattered the peaceful atmosphere. "He's gone! My son is gone!" Her voice echoed through the park, a desperate plea for help.

Zina's head snapped up, her tranquil demeanor replaced by a focused intensity. Her eyes scanned the crowd, searching for any sign of the missing child. "Do not worry," she said, her voice filled with a quiet confidence that belied the chaos around us. "I will find him."

She closed her eyes, her hands outstretched, palms facing upwards. A faint, ethereal glow emanated from her body, and I felt a surge of energy crackling in the air. When she opened her eyes, they were filled with a strange, luminous light.

"Follow me," she said, her voice barely a whisper, yet carrying an undeniable authority.

We weaved through the panicked crowd, Zina leading the way with an uncanny sense of direction. She moved with a purpose, her steps guided by an invisible force. Within minutes, we found ourselves standing before a large oak tree, its gnarled branches casting long shadows on the ground.

Zina knelt down, peering into the darkness beneath the tree. "It's okay," she said softly.. "Your parents are worried about you. Let's take you back to them."

A small figure emerged from the shadows, his face streaked with tears. The missing boy, his eyes wide with fear, clung to the tree trunk as if it were his lifeline.

Zina smiled, a warm, reassuring smile that melted the fear in the boy's eyes. "I promise," she said, her voice gentle, "everything will be alright."

She extended her hand, and the boy, hesitantly at first, reached out and took it. Zina led him back to his frantic parents, their faces etched with relief as they embraced their lost child.

As we walked away, the grateful parents' voices fading into the background, I couldn't help but feel a surge of pride. Zina had used her extraordinary powers for good, to reunite a family and bring a sense of peace to a chaotic situation.

"You were amazing back there," I said, my voice filled with genuine admiration. "You're like a superhero."

We continued our walk.

"You've changed." Zina observed, her voice filled with a warmth that melted away the last vestiges of my anxiety. "You are no longer the boy I met in the lab."

I smiled, a genuine smile that reached my eyes. "Yeah, I guess I have," I admitted, a sense of gratitude washing over me. "Meeting you has changed my life, Zina. You've opened my eyes to a world I never knew existed."

She nodded, her eyes filled with a wisdom.

ॐ

As we strolled through the park, a figure emerged from the shadows, blocking our path. He was tall and imposing, his broad shoulders and muscular build hinting at a formidable strength. His eyes, dark and piercing, burned with an intensity that sent shivers down my spine.

"Zina," he said, his voice a low growl that rumbled through the air. "I've been searching for you."

Zina stiffened beside me, her body radiating a protective energy. Her eyes narrowed, her voice sharp as a blade. "Who are you?" she demanded, her demeanor a stark contrast to the playful woman I had seen moments earlier.

"You very well know," the seeker replied, his voice a chilling echo in the tranquil park. "And I know you possess the Blue Rose."

VI

A New Dawn

My heart skipped a beat. The Blue Rose? What was that?

I glanced at Zina, but her face was an unreadable.

"I do not know what you are talking about," she said calmly, but I could sense the underlying tension in her voice, the steel beneath the silk.

The seeker let out a cold, mirthless laugh. "Don't play games with me, Zina," he warned, his gaze unwavering. "I know you have it. The key to Kaelumoor."

Zina's eyes flashed with anger, her serenity shattered. "You will not have it," she declared, her voice filled with a chilling resolve that sent a shiver down my spine.

Before I could even blink, Zina lunged at the seeker, her movements a blur of speed and grace. A whirlwind of energy erupted around them, obscuring their forms in a blinding flash of light. I stumbled backward, shielding my eyes from the intense brightness.

The air crackled with raw power as Zina unleashed a torrent of attacks. She moved with superhuman agility, her punches and kicks landing with devastating precision. The seeker, though clearly skilled, was no match for her. He struggled to defend himself, his movements growing increasingly desperate as Zina's relentless assault continued.

I watched in awe and terror as the battle raged, the park's peaceful atmosphere shattered by the clash of supernatural forces. The ground trembled beneath their feet, trees swayed violently, and the air hummed with an otherworldly energy.

Finally, Zina landed a decisive blow, a powerful kick that sent the seeker flying backward. He crashed into a nearby tree, his body crumpling to the ground. Zina seized the opportunity, her hand reaching out to grab him, their forms dissolving into thin air, leaving behind only a fading resound of their struggle.

I stood there, stunned, my heart pounding in my chest. The park was silent once more, the only sound the gentle rustling of leaves in the breeze. What had just happened? Where had they gone? And what was the Blue Rose? Was Zina safe? What would the seeker do to her if he caught her? The questions rang in my mind, unanswered and unsettling.

I took a deep breath, trying to steady my nerves. I had to trust Zina. She was strong, resourceful, and she had promised to protect me.

With a heavy heart, I turned and walked back to the mansion.

&

As I entered the house, Zina was already there, waiting for me. Her usual serenity had returned, but her eyes held a fierce resolve, a steely determination that sent a shiver down my spine.

"KD," she said, her voice urgent, "we must prepare. The time has come."

"We must find the Blue Rose" Zina said, her voice firm, a newfound urgency in her eyes. "Before they return."

"They?" I asked, my heart pounding like a drum. "You mean there are more of them?"

She nodded grimly. "They are relentless. They will stop at nothing to obtain the Blue Rose."

"But what is it?" I pressed, my curiosity piqued. "Why is it so important?"

Zina's gaze drifted towards the sprawling mansion, a flicker of understanding in her eyes. "It is here, KD," she revealed, her voice barely above a whisper. "In this house."

My jaw dropped. "Here? But how do you know?"

"I can sense its energy," she explained, her voice hushed. "It is calling to me."

A shiver ran down my spine. The Blue Rose, the key to Kaelumoor, was hidden somewhere within the walls of my own home. We had to find it, and fast.

"Let us begin." I declared.

The hours melted away, the mansion's secrets slowly unraveling before us. But the Blue Rose remained elusive, its hiding place a tantalizing mystery.

As the night wore on, a sense of desperation began to creep in. Where could it be? Had we missed something? Had my father been more cunning than we had anticipated?

Just as I was about to give up hope, Zina's hand shot out, stopping me in my tracks.

"There," she whispered, her eyes fixed on a section of the library wall.

I followed her gaze, but all I saw was a seemingly ordinary wall, adorned with intricate carvings and ornate moldings. She walked towards it, her fingers tracing the patterns on the wood.

Suddenly, she pressed her hand against a hidden panel, and with a soft click, the wall slid open, revealing a hidden chamber.

The hidden chamber wasn't just a room; it was a clandestine laboratory, a testament to my father's secret life. It was smaller than the main lab where we had found Zina, but it pulsated with a more potent, almost sinister energy. Rows of beakers and vials lined the shelves, their contents glowing with an eerie luminescence that cast long shadows across the walls. Strange, humming machines occupied the workbenches, their purpose shrouded in mystery.

This must have been the lab my dad built with Charlie's father, the one mentioned in the contract. A cold shiver ran down my spine as I recognized some of the chemicals.. the same ones I had researched online, the ones capable of unimaginable destruction.

In the center of the room, a massive steel locker gleamed under the harsh fluorescent lights. It was clearly high-tech, its surface smooth and impenetrable, with a keypad and a biometric scanner guarding its contents.

"This is it," Zina whispered, her voice filled with a mixture of awe and trepidation. "The Blue Rose must be inside."

"It's protected," she said, a hint of frustration in her voice. "We need a way to open it."

I racked my brain, desperation gnawing at me. We were so close, yet so far. Suddenly, a thought struck me, a desperate gamble that might just pay off.

"Zina," I said, my voice trembling with excitement, "try my biometrics."

She looked at me, puzzled. "Are you sure?"

I nodded, my heart pounding in my chest. "The scanner. It might be programmed to recognize my dad and since I'm his son... maybe it would work.. if that makes any sense!"

And it WORKED!!

As Zina reached inside the locker, her delicate fingers brushing against the cool metal, my eyes darted around the lab. My gaze fell upon a dusty shelf, cluttered with beakers and test tubes. Something caught my eye, a small, rectangular object tucked away behind a row of glassware.

With a trembling hand, I pulled it out. It was a photograph, its edges frayed and yellowed with age. The picture showed me as a baby, my father holding me in his arms, a proud smile on his face. But it was the figure standing beside him that made my blood run cold.

It was Charlie. A young girl, no older than ten, with a mischievous grin and sparkling eyes. My heart pounded in my chest. This was impossible. Charlie, the ruthless crime lord, the woman who held the city in her iron grip, had been a part of my childhood?

I couldn't reconcile the image in the photograph with the woman I had met just days earlier. The innocent girl with the playful grin couldn't possibly be the same person as the cold, calculating criminal who threatened Zina and held my fate in her hands.

But the evidence was undeniable. There they were, side-by-side, my father and a young Charlie, their smiles hinting at a shared history.

I was confused. What did this mean? Had my father been involved in Charlie's criminal activities? Was he complicit in her dark deeds? The questions swirled in my mind, a tempest of doubt and fear.

Zina emerged from the locker, her face illuminated by a soft, ethereal glow. In her hands, she held the Blue Rose, its iridescent surface shimmering with an otherworldly light. The stone pulsed with energy, a tangible power that hummed in the air around us.

"We have it," she whispered, her voice filled with awe and reverence.

The Blue Rose, the key to Kaelumoor, was finally in our possession. But the weight of its power, the responsibility it carried, pressed down on me like a mountain. We had what we came for, but the journey was far from over.

ॐ

Zina's head snapped up, her eyes narrowing with a steely resolve. "They're here," she said, her voice a chilling whisper. "We must protect the Blue Rose."

We rushed out of the lab, the Blue Rose clutched tightly in Zina's hand, its ethereal glow casting long shadows on the walls. As we emerged into the hallway, a group of figures materialized from the darkness, their forms shimmering and shifting like oil on water. They were the seekers, their eyes burning with an insatiable hunger, their presence a suffocating wave of malice.

Without hesitation, Zina charged forward, a warrior princess defending her kingdom. The Blue Rose pulsed in her hand, its energy radiating outwards, forming a protective shield around her. The seekers lunged, their movements swift and predatory, their claws and fangs bared in a silent snarl.

A fierce battle erupted with the clash of supernatural forces. Furniture was overturned, paintings ripped from the walls, and the once pristine mansion became a war zone. Zina moved with a grace and power that belied her delicate frame. She dodged and weaved, her movements a mesmerizing dance of death. Her hands glowed with an ethereal light, unleashing bursts of energy that sent the seekers reeling backward.

I watched in awe and terror as the battle raged around me. I wanted to help, but I knew I would only be a liability. My human strength and agility were no match for these otherworldly creatures. All I could do was watch, my heart pounding in my chest, my breath caught in my throat.

The seekers fought with a relentless ferocity, their numbers seemingly endless. They attacked from all sides, their claws tearing at Zina's defenses, their fangs snapping at her heels. But Zina was undeterred. She fought with the fury of a cornered animal, her determination fueled by the need to protect the Blue Rose.

THE BATTLE RAGED ON!

One by one, Zina dispatched the seekers, their bodies dissolving into wisps of shadow as they fell. But their numbers seemed endless, a relentless tide of darkness crashing against her defenses.

Zina fought on, her movements gradually slowing, her breaths coming in ragged gasps. Exhaustion etched itself onto her face, but her eyes blazed with an unyielding determination.

Finally, the last seeker fell, its form dissolving into nothingness, leaving a lingering silence in the ravaged hallway. Zina stood amidst the wreckage, her shoulders slumped, her chest heaving with exertion. The Blue Rose, still clutched tightly in her hand, pulsed with a soft, reassuring glow.

Just as the dust began to settle, a new figure emerged from the shadows. My heart leaped into my throat as I recognized the familiar silhouette. It was my dad, his face pale and drawn, his eyes wide with disbelief.

"KD?" he asked, his voice a hoarse whisper. "What's going on here? What's all this mess?"

He surveyed the scene before him, the overturned furniture, the shattered glass, the lingering traces of otherworldly energy. His gaze fell upon Zina, recognition crossing his face.

The silence stretched, heavy with unspoken questions and a lifetime of secrets. The moment of truth had arrived.

I opened my mouth, my heart pounding. How could I explain the unexplainable? How could I bridge the gap between my father's ordinary world and the extraordinary reality Zina had brought into our lives? The words tangled in my throat, a jumble of fear and confusion.

Before I could utter a sound, Zina stepped forward, her eyes locked on my father. Her demeanor had shifted, the warmth and gentleness replaced by a chilling coldness.

"Kael D'Souza," she said, her voice sharp as a shard of ice.

My dad's eyes widened in recognition, his face draining of color. "Zina?" he whispered, his voice barely audible, a mixture of shock and disbelief.

In that instant, the atmosphere charged with an otherworldly energy. Zina's expression hardened, her eyes blazing with a fury I had never seen before. It was a primal rage, a storm of emotions that threatened to consume everything in its path.

She raised her hand, her fingers outstretched, and a blinding light engulfed the room. I screamed, instinctively shielding my eyes from the searing brightness. The world around me dissolved into a swirling vortex of white, a blinding void that erased all sense of reality.

When the light finally faded, I dared to open my eyes. The scene before me was one of utter devastation. The hallway was in ruins, the walls scorched, the furniture reduced to charred fragments.

And my dad was gone.

I stumbled back, my legs weak, my mind reeling. My dad was gone, vanished without a trace, leaving behind only a blinding light. Zina stood amidst the wreckage, her eyes filled with a profound sadness, a grief that mirrored my own.

ॐ

"I'm sorry." Zina whispered, her voice heavy with regret. "It had to be done."

A million questions burned on my tongue, but the words wouldn't come. My throat constricted, choked by a grief I had never known. All I could do was stare at the empty space where my father had stood moments before, a gaping wound in the fabric of my reality.

Zina reached out to comfort me, her hand hovering tentatively near my arm. But I flinched away, my body recoiling from her touch. The pain was too raw, too fresh. How could she do this? How could she take my father from me?

"KD," she said softly, her voice filled with a sorrow that mirrored my own. "I never wanted to hurt you. But I had to protect my people."

I shook my head, tears blurring my vision. "My dad... he was my dad," I choked out, the words barely a whisper.

Zina's eyes softened, her expression filled with a deep empathy. "I know," she said, her voice barely audible. "And I am truly sorry."

She stepped back, her gaze falling on the Blue Rose, which now lay on the floor, its light dimmed. With a trembling hand, she picked it up and whispered an ancient incantation, the words flowing from her lips like a forgotten melody. The stone pulsed with a blinding light, engulfing her in its brilliance.

In a flash, she was gone, leaving me alone in the silent lab. The Blue Rose had vanished, and so had Zina.

ജ

I was left standing there, numb with shock and grief. My world had been shattered, the pieces scattered like broken glass. My father, my home, my sense of normalcy - all gone.

The weight of loss pressed down on me, a crushing burden that threatened to suffocate me. I sank to the floor, tears streaming down my face, my sobs reverberating in the empty room. My heart ached with a pain I had never known, a pain that cut deeper than any physical wound.

I was alone, truly alone. Zina's words reverberated in my mind, a haunting reminder of the sacrifices made in the name of a greater good. But in that moment, all I could feel was the emptiness, the gaping void left by the absence of my father.

My life had been turned upside down, and I didn't know how to pick up the pieces.

(the saga continues...)

A Note From Author

Writing this book has been an incredible journey. I hope you enjoyed reading it as much as I enjoyed writing it. If you liked the story, please consider leaving a review or telling your friends about it. I'd love to hear what you think!

Abhinay Krishna.

Connect with the author:

Instagram:

@abhinaykrishna_ov / @abhinaywrites

Email:

connect@abhinaykrishna.com

Website:

www.abhinaykrishna.com / www.abhinaywrites.blog

<u>*Notes for Reader:*</u>

Notes for Reader:

Notes for Reader:

Notes for Reader:

Notes for Reader: